The House That Drac Built

WRITTEN BY JUDY SIERRA

ILLUSTRATED BY WILL HILLENBRAND

GULLIVER BOOKS

HARCOURT BRACE & COMPANY

SAN DIEGO   NEW YORK   LONDON

Library of Congress Cataloging-in-Publication Data
Sierra, Judy.
The house that Drac built/Judy Sierra; illustrated by Will Hillenbrand.—1st ed.
p. cm.
"Gulliver Books."
Summary: In this Halloween version of a familiar cumulative rhyme,
the inhabitants of a haunted house get increasingly agitated
until a group of children sets things right.
ISBN 0-15-201069-6
[1. Haunted houses—Fiction. 2. Halloween—Fiction. 3. Stories in rhyme.]
I. Hillenbrand, Will, ill. II. Title.
PZ8.3.S577HO 1995
[E]—dc20 94-19002

Printed in Singapore
Special Edition for Scholastic Book Fairs, Inc.
A C E F D B

The illustrations in this book were done in oil and oil pastel on paper.
The display type was hand rendered by Judythe Sieck.
The text type was set in Nicholas Cochin.
Color separations were made by Bright Arts, Ltd., Singapore.
Printed and bound by Tien Wah Press, Singapore
This book was printed on Leykam recycled paper,
which contains more than 20 percent postconsumer waste
and has a total recycled content of at least 50 percent.
Production supervision by Warren Wallerstein and Ginger Boyer
Designed by Kaelin Chappell and Will Hillenbrand

To Jan and Don Lieberman
—J. S.

To Jane, Liz, Kaelin, and Benjamin
—W. H.

This is the house that Drac built.

This is the bat
that lived in the house that Drac built.

This is the cat
that bit the bat
that lived in the house that Drac built.

This is the werewolf
that chased the cat
that bit the bat
that lived in the house that Drac built.

This is the fearsome manticore
that wrestled the werewolf
that chased the cat
that bit the bat
that lived in the house that Drac built.

This is the monster whose bloodcurdling roar
startled the fearsome manticore
that wrestled the werewolf
that chased the cat
that bit the bat
that lived in the house that Drac built.

This is the coffin under the floor
that fell on the monster whose bloodcurdling roar
startled the fearsome manticore
that wrestled the werewolf
that chased the cat
that bit the bat
that lived in the house that Drac built.

This is the mummy from days of yore
that rose from the coffin under the floor
that fell on the monster whose bloodcurdling roar
startled the fearsome manticore
that wrestled the werewolf
that chased the cat
that bit the bat
that lived in the house that Drac built.

This is the zombie famous in lore
that unwrapped the mummy from days of yore
that rose from the coffin under the floor
that fell on the monster whose bloodcurdling roar
startled the fearsome manticore
that wrestled the werewolf
that chased the cat
that bit the bat
that lived in the house that Drac built.

This is the fiend of Bloodygore
that served the zombie famous in lore
that unwrapped the mummy from days of yore
that rose from the coffin under the floor
that fell on the monster whose bloodcurdling roar

startled the fearsome manticore
that wrestled the werewolf
that chased the cat
that bit the bat
that lived in the house that Drac built.

These are the children who knocked at the door . . .

and frightened the fiend of Bloodygore
and zapped the zombie famous in lore.

They rewrapped the mummy from days of yore
and closed the coffin under the floor
and shushed the monster's bloodcurdling roar.

They soothed the fearsome manticore
and caged the werewolf
and petted the cat
and bandaged the bat . . .

that lived in the house that Drac built.